W9-CBX-757

I HAD A FAVORITE DRESS

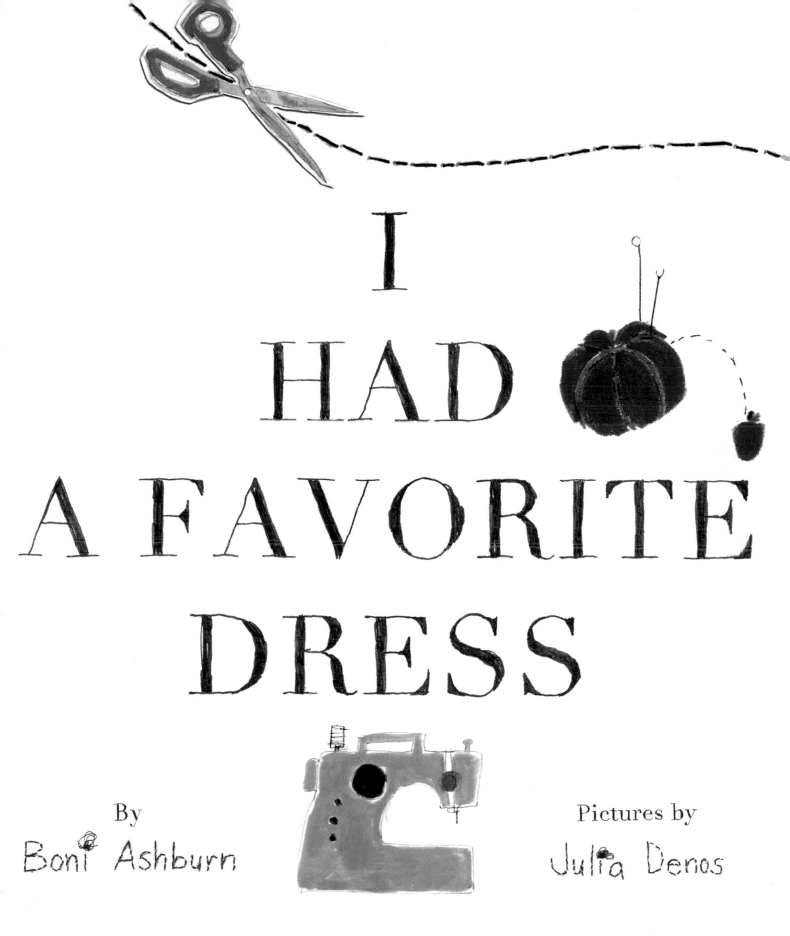

By
Boni Ashburn

Pictures by
Julia Denos

Abrams Books for Young Readers
New York

For Lily,
my favoritest girly girl
—B.A.

For my littlest sister, Shauna,
with love, admiration,
and hand-me-downs
—J.D.

But one Tuesday, I put on my favorite dress . . .

and it was too short! Mama said so. Uh-oh!

I couldn't bear the thought of not wearing my favoritest

dress. So I moaned and I groaned, I complained, distraught . . .

"You're overwrought, dear, it's clear," Mama said. "Don't make

mountains out of molehills. Make molehills out of mountains."

Well, that wasn't very clear at *all*, I thought,
but why not *make* something out of my dress?
So I asked my mama, "Mama, dear . . ."

And SNIP, SNIP, SNIP,

Sew, Sew, Sew...

New shirt,

hello!

And my new ruffly shirt became
my favoritest shirt, and I wore it every
Wednesday, because that was
my *new* favorite day of the week.

But one warm Wednesday, I put on my favorite shirt . . . and the sleeves were too tight! Mama said so. Uh-oh!

Well, it took a lot less thought that time for things to become clear . . .

So I asked my mama, "Mama, dear . . ."

And

SNIP, SNIP,

Sew, Sew...

Tank top,

hello!

And my new easy-breezy tank top became my
Thursday tank top (because Thursdays
are always the *hottest* summer days), and I wore it
every Thursday until . . .

School! No tank tops, it's the rule.
So I asked my mama, "Mama, dear . . ."

And SNIP, SNIP,

Sew,
Sew...

New skirt,

hello!

And my new cool-for-school skirt looked *just right* with my favorite tights! I wore it one Friday, and it *felt* just right, so I wore it every Friday (my *new* favorite day of the week!).

Until the Friday that Maggie Jean (the Fashion Queen
and my very bestest friend) said it was the *end* for skirts!

"Without a doubt," she declared, "pants are *in* and
skirts are *out*!"

But it was OK, don't you know,

'cause just about then it started to snow.

I showed my dear mama the snow. "Mama, see . . . "

And

SNIP,
SNIP,

Sew,

Sew...

Tassely scarf,

hello!

And my scarf became my favoritest thing
to wear every snowy Saturday,
the best play-in-the-snow day,
until the day . . .

. . . my tassely scarf got caught in the door.
Uh-oh! The long, swaying ends (that were now
short and frayed) no longer swayed to and fro.

At first I felt tears till I shook my head clear
and showed my new problem to Mama dear . . .

SNIP,
SNIP,

Sew,
Sew...

Pair of socks,

hello!

I slipped those socks on my feet every Sunday,
which was my *new* favoritest day of the week.

Because on Sundays, we go to Grandma's house with
the white-on-white wall-to-wall carpet, and Grandma's
eyebrows silently invite us to remove our shoes.

Why, hello, nifty new socks!

Until a Sunday, in the morn,
when I found one sock, forlorn. Uh-oh!
Mama said, "It's very clear there's not much left
of your dear, departed dress!"

SNIP, SNIP, sew, sew...

Pretty hair bow,

hello!

It held my hair back on the windiest days, on the swingiest swings, and through my twirliest twirls in ballet class.

My hair bow, my pretty hair bow, was my favoritest accessory, worn for all the world to see, on **Mondays**, which are the *best* days 'cause the week is new and shiny, until . . .

My puppy, my *chewy* puppy, with the tiniest,
sharpest teeth the world has ever seen, chewed
my pretty hair bow into the tiniest scraps of fabric
I'd ever seen!

"Puppy, no!" Uh-oh. It was a bow no more.

But by *now*, I knew not to have a *cow*
when things go wrong.

I scooped up those scraps and bits of my
Tuesday dress, the favoritest dress I'd ever had,
and made . . .

. . . this!

Now I can wear my favoritest dress
every day of every season of every year!

I showed my mama, who said, "How
wonderful, dear!"

And she smiled and said something about mountains and molehills again, which still wasn't clear . . .

And *then* she looked me up and down with squinty eyes and added, "Don't panic, my dear, but I fear . . . those *pants* look a little too short . . ."
UH-OH!